DINOSAUR TRACKER!

WWW.JURASSICWORLD.COM

Jurassic World: Fallen Kingdom is a trademark
and copyright of Universal Studios and Amblin
Entertainment, Inc. All Rights Reserved.

RANDOM HOUSE 🏠 NEW YORK

By Rachel Chlebowski

rhcbooks.com
ISBN 978-0-525-58081-2 (trade) — ISBN 978-0-525-58082-9 (ebook)
Printed in the United States of America
Designed by Diane Choi
10 9 8 7 6 5 4 3 2 1

JURASSIC WORLD was once the most amazing theme park in the world—with living dinosaurs! But after the dinosaurs escaped, the park was destroyed and the island was abandoned, leaving the dinosaurs to live in the wild, as they once did millions of years ago.

Now a big volcano on the island has roared back to life, so the dinosaurs need YOUR help! Use this book as a guide to track and save these amazing creatures before time runs out on them again!

VELOCIRAPTOR

SEC 4

LAT : 75° 55' 15" RDA : 962
LON : 35° 20' 15" ARCSEC P: 26.3

TRACKER 1

Blue is considered the most intelligent dinosaur at Jurassic World. A *Velociraptor* with six-inch razor-sharp claws on each hand, Blue is also extremely dangerous! *Velociraptors* are quick and silent, so keep an eye out for this creature at all times. If you're not hunting her, she's probably already hunting you!

AGGRESSION INDEX:	NAME MEANING:	ORIGINAL HABITAT:
VERY HIGH	"Swift thief"	Mongolia

LENGTH:	WEIGHT:	STANCE:
11 ft.	130 lbs.	Biped

DIET:	AGE: Early Cretaceous,
Carnivore	115–108 million years ago

TYRANNOSAURUS REX

The *Tyrannosaurus rex* is one of the most fearsome dinosaurs ever to walk the earth. One bite from a *T. rex* can easily crush a school bus! This carnivore ruled the island when the park was abandoned, and she shouldn't be hard to find—but she's very difficult to catch!

STANCE: Biped

ORIGINAL HABITAT: Western North America

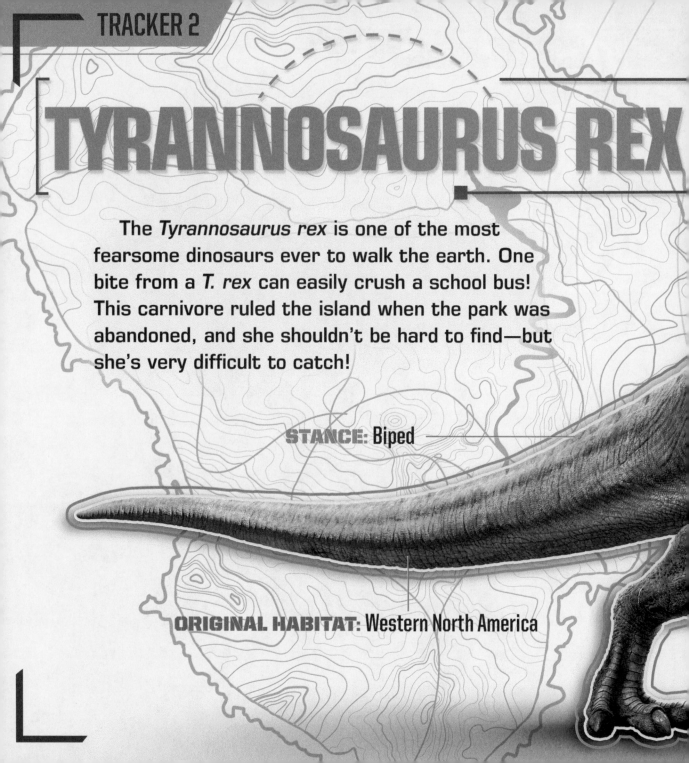

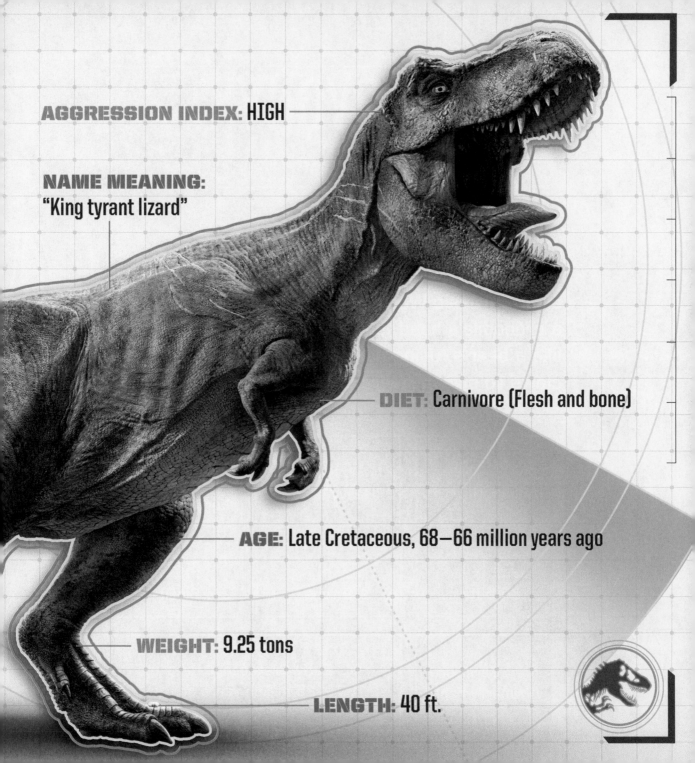

AGGRESSION INDEX: HIGH

NAME MEANING: "King tyrant lizard"

DIET: Carnivore (Flesh and bone)

AGE: Late Cretaceous, 68–66 million years ago

WEIGHT: 9.25 tons

LENGTH: 40 ft.

BARYONYX

LAT : 25° 65' 15"   RDA : 162
LON : 35° 70' 15"   ARCSEC P: 53.3

SEC 1

TRACKER 3

Baryonyx is the largest fish-eating dinosaur in all of Jurassic World. Although her head looks like a crocodile's head, she has a hunting style more like a bear's, using her powerful and dangerous claws to sweep rivers and lakes for tasty fish.

AGGRESSION INDEX: HIGH

NAME MEANING: "Heavy claw"

ORIGINAL HABITAT: River deltas of Europe

LENGTH: 30.5 ft.

WEIGHT: 1.9 tons

STANCE: Biped

DIET: Carnivore (Primarily fish)

AGE: Early Cretaceous, 130–125 million years ago

STATUS://

MIT SLPNG: 12 59 78 146 78

LUMA RANGES

SPLIT SOURCE

LOCATION: 15_79_78 93P [ACTIVE]

TR-03-EGG

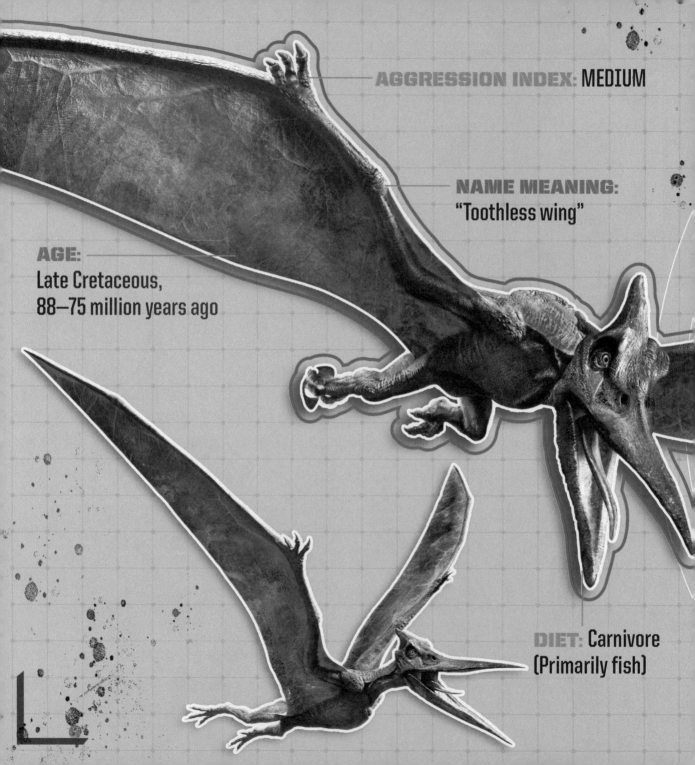

AGGRESSION INDEX: MEDIUM

NAME MEANING:
"Toothless wing"

AGE:
Late Cretaceous,
88–75 million years ago

DIET: Carnivore
(Primarily fish)

PTERANODON

Pteranodons are the largest *Pterosaurs,* or flying reptiles, at Jurassic World—with wingspans wider than those of any known bird. Beware: *Pteranodons* have been known to land on humans—and with three clawed fingers on each hand and four clawed toes on each foot, these flying creatures can cause a lot of damage.

WINGSPAN: Over 20 ft.

WEIGHT: 6.6 lbs.

STANCE: Quadruped/Winged

ORIGINAL HABITAT:
North America, Europe

CARNOTAURUS

LAT : 95° 52' 25"   RDA : 762
LON : 25° 30' 15"   ARCSEC P: 62.6

SEC 3

TRACKER 5

The *Carnotaurus* looks like a smaller version of the *Tyrannosaurus rex*, but with one major difference—she has horns like a bull! This speedy dinosaur is capable of chasing and eating other dinosaurs, although her small skull may keep her from attacking the larger plant-eaters.

AGGRESSION INDEX: HIGH

NAME MEANING: "Meat-eating bull"

HABITAT: South America

LENGTH: 34 ft.

WEIGHT: 2.3 tons

STANCE: Biped

DIET: Carnivore (Small to medium prey, including turtles and smaller dinosaurs)

AGE: Late Cretaceous, 72–69 million years ago

BLOOD SAMPLES

SAMPLE 01

SAMPLE 02

SAMPLE 03

SAMPLE 04

SAMPLE 06

ANKYLOSAURUS

Paleontologists have called the *Ankylosaurus* a living tank due to the spiky armor that runs from her skull to the rounded club at the end of her tail. This dinosaur is a plant-eater, but she's built to survive against much larger predators, such as the *T. rex* or *Carnotaurus*.

DIET: Herbivore (Ferns and other low-growing vegetation)

NAME MEANING: "Fused lizard"

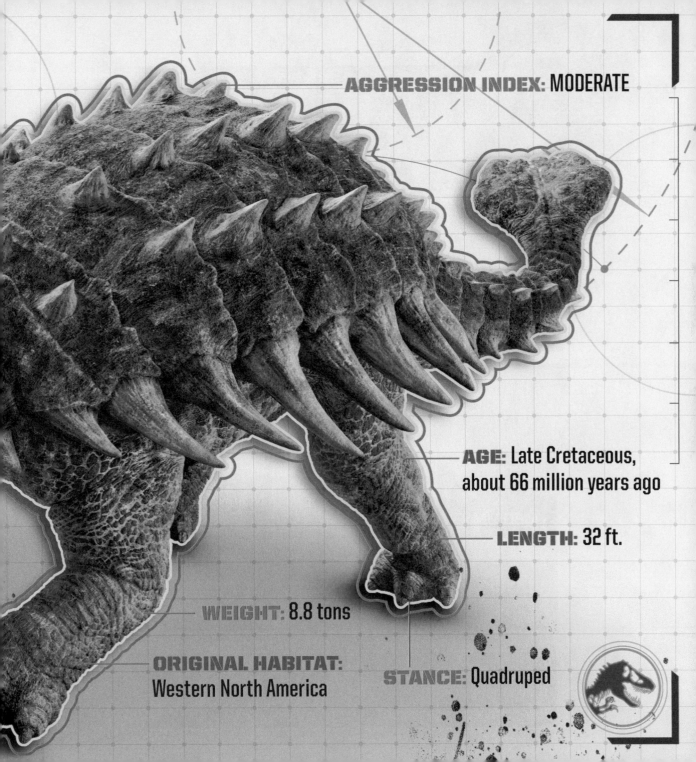

AGGRESSION INDEX: MODERATE

AGE: Late Cretaceous, about 66 million years ago

LENGTH: 32 ft.

WEIGHT: 8.8 tons

STANCE: Quadruped

ORIGINAL HABITAT: Western North America

STYGIMOLOCH

SEC 5

LAT : 75° 25' 52"   RDA : 622
LON : 95° 30' 15"   ARCSEC P: 76.6

TRACKER 7

The *Stygimoloch* is a small herbivore that weighs as much as an adult human and is about as long as a car and as fast as an ostrich! She can be recognized by her incredibly thick skull, as well as by the knobs on her snout. Even though the Stiggy is small, that doesn't mean she isn't tough. Because what the Stiggy lacks in size, she greatly makes up for in courage!

AGGRESSION INDEX:
MEDIUM

NAME MEANING:
"River Styx demon"

ORIGINAL HABITAT:
Mainly North America

LENGTH:
7.2 ft.

WEIGHT:
200 lbs.

STANCE:
Biped

DIET: Herbivore (Ferns and other low-growing vegetation)

AGE: Late Cretaceous, 68–66 million years ago

BACKUP POWER
CORE: 100%

AGGRESSION INDEX: MODERATE

NAME MEANING: "Roofed lizard"

ORIGINAL HABITAT:
North America

LENGTH: 33 ft.

WEIGHT: 3.8 tons

STANCE: Quadruped

DIET: Herbivore (Ferns and other low-growing vegetation)

AGE: Late Jurassic, about 150 million years ago

STEGOSAURUS

With broad, bony plates running from her neck down to her back, the *Stegosaurus* was one of the most popular dinosaur attractions at Jurassic World before the park shut down. This dinosaur may be an unaggressive herbivore, but beware her dangerous tail and the four long spikes at the end of it!

TRICERATOPS
SEC 2

LAT : 15° 55' 75"   RDA : 262
LON : 26° 20' 15"   ARCSEC P: 75.3

TRACKER 9

Triceratops is by far the largest of the horned dinosaurs. Although these dinosaurs dine mostly on shoots and leaves, they can easily trample a human or hurt them with their horns, so always keep a safe distance—or you might pay the price!

AGGRESSION INDEX: HIGH

NAME MEANING: "Three-horned face"

ORIGINAL HABITAT: Western North America

LENGTH: 26 ft.

WEIGHT: 11 tons

STANCE: Quadruped

DIET: Herbivore (Ferns and other low-growing vegetation)

AGE: Late Cretaceous, 68—66 million years ago

INDORAPTOR

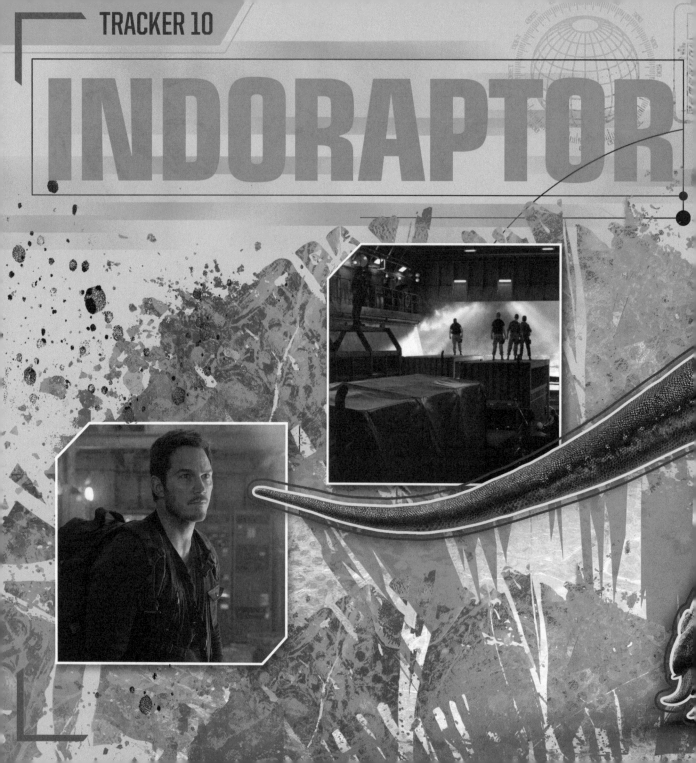

The scientists of Jurassic World also created new breeds of dinosaurs—don't be surprised if you come across something that has never been seen before! Some of these creatures may have gotten away. Anything that survives the destruction of the island should be considered extremely dangerous.

DANGER!

Our mission is to save these amazing creatures from extinction, and we can't do that unless we come back alive—so safety first! Pack your bags and get ready for the adventure of a lifetime!

TRACKER 3

N E S W

JURASSIC WORLD
FALLEN KINGDOM

DINOSAUR TRACKER
MAIN SYSTEM · ISLA NUBLAR   NGC 6240

ISLA NUBLAR

TRACKER 4

TRACKER 2
SEC 4

TRACKER 3
SEC 4

JURASSIC WORLD
FALLEN KINGDOM

ISLA
NUBLAR

04

Jurassic World™ & © Universal Studios and Amblin Entertainment, Inc.

DINOSAUR TRACKER!

DINOSAUR TRACKER!

DINOSAUR TRACKER!

DINOSAUR TRACKER!

DINOSAUR TRACKER!

DINOSAUR TRACKER!

ANKYLOSAURUS

MOSASAURUS

PTERANODON

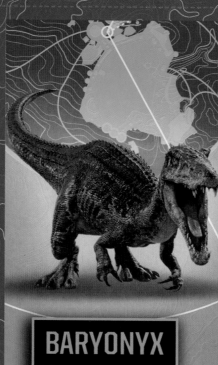

BARYONYX

INDORAPTOR

STYGIMOLOCH

BLUE

CARNOTAURUS

T. REX

TRICERATOPS

STEGOSAURUS